Claiming the She-Wolf

Black Hills Wolves
Book 23

By

Louisa Bacio

Copyright © 2016 by Louisa Bacio
ISBN: 978-1-61333-971-8
Cover art by Fiona Jayde

Published by Decadent Publishing Company, LLC
Look for us online at:
www.decadentpublishing.com

Reviews for *Claiming the She-Wolf*

The chemistry sizzles between Tala and Yaz, and they leave you begging for more ~ VampireRomanceBooks.com

Good characters, spicy sex scenes and all the goodness that comes from reading a Louisa Bacio book. You can't go wrong ~ Amazon Reviewer

Yas Collins and Tala Graystone have their story to tell and it's told beautifully. They are an amazing couple and this is the type of feel good story I needed to read ~ Amazon Reviewer

Their attraction is off the charts and loved the build to their sexy times ~ Amazon Reviewer

Could not put this book down! ~ Amazon Reviewer

~A Note from Louisa Bacio~

Welcome to the Wolf's Lair B&B. By now, you've probably gotten to know our quaint but growing town of Los Lobos, and I can't wait for you to meet Tala and Yas.

Yas returns to town a bit of an outsider, with a mission of discovering his birthplace and to tame his inner wolf. But it'll take a feisty she-wolf to fully bring out the beast before he can get his shifting under control.

While you're here, you may run into a few familiar faces, and maybe discover some new ones.

Many thanks go out to Rebecca Royce, who started the pack of the Black Hills Wolves authors, along with Heather Long, and to Kerry Adrienne for suggesting my initiation.

Get ready to run in the wild, and I hope you enjoy the journey.

I'm always happy to hear from readers. You can contact me at Louisa@LouisaBacio.com

Dedication

To all those who like to howl at the full moon.

Chapter One

The house shook from the thunder, and Tala's body shuddered. She didn't want to go through another storm in this hellhole. Mostly because she doubted it could weather another one.

"What makes you think you can run a business?" Lightning flashed, illuminating the anger on her brother's face. The generator ran out of fuel about an hour before, and with the storm, they wouldn't be able to refill before daylight.

"I sure the hell excel at cooking and cleaning, better than you do at keeping the generator running," Tala said, keeping her voice even and calm. He wouldn't goad her into a blowout. "You made sure I knew how to do that."

He pushed off the wall and stalked forward. "It's much different, little sister." He put his index and middle finger under her chin and tilted it upward to have her look into his eyes. "I don't think you have what it takes to run this place."

She shook off his hands and retreated behind the counter, using it as a barrier between her and him. His nostrils flared, a sure sign of his anger.

"Who will look after you if I leave you here alone? Who's going to take care of you?"

She stifled a laugh. As if he could even manage to put food on the table. *Come on.* He probably worried more about who'd feed him if she didn't go with him.

Holding her ground, she stared directly into his eyes. "I'll manage."

Her challenge hung between them, so tangible she could pluck it from the air and eat it. But fuck it. Who said she always had to be the one to concede? Not this time. Los Lobos had been her home her entire life, and no way in hell she wanted to leave, not when the rebuilding had started. Why didn't Shilah see things the way she did?

They came from the same blood. It had to be worth something.

"It's not safe for you here, and it's my duty to take care of you."

She shook her head. It didn't matter how much things changed, some built-in prejudices remained. As the eldest and the male, her brother thought he should be head of the household, and she needed to obey. She'd learned a long time ago how to control him.

"Listen, you've got a great opportunity ahead of you—college. It's only for a little while. Go learn and then come back home. I'll be fine. I have the support of the pack."

He barely withheld his snort of contempt. "The pack? Right. As if you've been chosen as a mate. More like a maid servant than a maid-in-waiting."

Her emotions bristled at his unkind words. At twenty-four, she wasn't treading old-maid waters yet, but the waterfall threatened right around the bend. She'd had a few suitors, but sometimes it was difficult to take a male that she'd known for most of their lives seriously. Especially when they went through the shifting transition. Boy could they be assholes.

Shilah tucked a wayward strand of her long black

hair behind her ear. "Why don't you get some rest? I need to finish packing a few things, and we can talk in the morning."

Their father had taken off when they were young, and she didn't remember him. After their mother died when Tala was seventeen, Shilah acted as her guardian. She'd miss him when he left, but the separation seemed best for both of them. Some distance would do them good.

"I won't change my mind," she insisted. She tossed her hair, knocking the strands loose again. "A night of sleep isn't going to bash some sense into me."

He slumped his shoulders with a sigh. "You are one handful. I feel sorry for whatever wolf eventually wins your heart. As they say, opposites attract. Maybe you'll find someone levelheaded with patience."

"As if. I'm not looking for a mate anytime soon."

***

Yas shifted the weight of his hiking pack. For the past mile, it had been rubbing on his lower back, and the repetition chafed a raw mark on his skin. Up ahead lay the outskirts of the town. As much as his mother had talked about it over the years, Los Lobos had taken on mythic proportions. He'd been young when his mother fled. The chaos of the old regime made her fear for their safety. Since the old crazy pack leader Magnum Tao had died, and his son Drew had taken over, there was talk that it was a better environment.

For a male Wolf coming into his own season, each shift varied. Yas avoided thinking about the way his hormones flared when the full moon came out. The few days beforehand, he was about useless. It got to the point where he couldn't be around women— she-wolf or human—or else he'd rip their clothes off and want to plow into them.

His last girlfriend didn't appreciate the overzealous lovemaking. He never took her against her will. She was more than willing to sleep with him, and they had on numerous occasions beforehand. When that time struck, she said it seemed he was elsewhere—doing her physically but not really being

5

there mentally. Like he was fantasizing about someone else. Truth be told, it wasn't some celebrity actress or pop star grinding her way through his mind. He'd been thinking about running in the wild, with the scent of the forest surrounding him and the clear open sky above. When he found a mate, they'd lay together in the grass, getting wet in the nighttime dew, soft mud cushioning their bodies. He stopped to adjust himself. Just thinking about the possibilities got him off.

Nope, the ex didn't appreciate his mental wanderings at all. So maybe the woman in his fantasies didn't resemble his former girlfriend. Instead of being blonde and fair-skinned like him, her darker skin shone under the moonlight, and he couldn't figure out what was the more black—her eyes or her hair.

The *caw-caw-caw* of a bluebird broke through the silence. What he'd give to crash in a cool, air-conditioned restaurant and take a load off. His white ass didn't appreciate the hot temps, and the sunscreen he'd put on made him sticky. He rounded the bend to the oasis of the small hidden town. He pushed past Gee's Bar and the convenience store. If he stopped now, he probably wouldn't make it to his destination until the sun went down. The Wolf he'd run into at the last watering hole filled him in on the changes in town, and directed him to a new place in town accepting boarders. He was promised better food and quieter quarters than Gee's Bar.

Taking a slug from his canteen, he swore to return to the bar for refreshments later and continued on. Dust coated his hiking boots, and a few new rips from slips and falls marred his jeans. Hopefully, the proprietor of the bed-and-breakfast wouldn't be so picky about renters because he'd not make a good first impression.

The road curved upward, taking a jarring left-hand turn before careening off into the forest. Although he'd been hiking through it, he stood for a moment, enjoying the tranquility and fresh air. No chain coffee shops or fast food drive-thrus in sight. People said things were not the same as they used to be. He bet none of them had even heard of Los

Lobos.

A pounding drew his attention. Before he discerned where it originated, he was given another clue.

"Dammit. You son of a bitch!" A woman with hips and curves aplenty hopped about in front of a makeshift flagpole. One hand swung a hammer, and she stuck the thumb of the other one into her mouth. He recognized the feeling. Sometimes with unexpected pain—like hitting one's thumb with a hammer—the cursing and walking in circles made him feel better. He'd actually read a study that said males who cursed and became physical tended to get over it faster than others.

"Need any help there?" he called out.

She turned toward his voice, and he sucked in a breath at her beauty. Sharp black-onyx eyes sparkled in frustration, and her red mouth stretched taught in a frown. One slash of bright blue streaked through her straight hair as black as a raven's wing.

"Don't need any help." She sized him up, from his muddy boots to his torn jeans and back to his face, which he knew had to be red and splotchy. "Especially help from a stranger."

Hefting the hammer with one hand, she held up the sign with the other. She swung at the nail, only to hit it at an angle and bend it.

"For crying out loud, can't I catch a break?" She tossed the hammer to the ground, bull's-eyeing two flowers that appeared to have recently been planted. Colored petals rained on the tilled dirt. "Great, just great."

Yas set down his pack, and he sighed with relief. If this woman was the proprietor of the bed-and-breakfast, he hoped to win over her approval. His appearance wasn't going to do it for him, and he wasn't carrying too much money. He didn't have a college savings account he could cash out and travel. His game plan was to work for his room and board.

With a watch on her movements, he picked up the hammer and used the claw end to remove the bent nail. "Do you have more nails?"

She eyed him and glanced at the house, as if judging how fast she could get to it if needed. "We don't get many strangers. What brings you to these parts?"

He smiled and hoped it didn't appear creepy or threatening. "My ma's from Los Lobos. Came to check out my roots. I'm looking for a place to stay for a few days."

The sign she'd been trying to hang read The Wolf's Lair B&B.

"Humpf." She dug into the front pocket of her coveralls and handed over a box of nails. "Hang that sign right, and I might be able to help you there."

The feeling of unease trapped in his chest dissipated. He stuck a few nails between his front teeth to hold them, and rammed in the ones holding up the signage. She handed over a second red piece of wood, *Vacancy*, which he hung off the bottom.

"Imagine that, a man who can use tools. I could have done it myself."

Warning signs flagged. He'd grown up with a single mother and younger sister, Sugar. Both fought often for their independence and got angry when he was able to open a jar they couldn't. His mom had never remarried, although she dated some. He figured she never wanted to lose control of her life. She'd run once, and that was enough.

"I don't doubt it," he said. "Still, I'm glad to have helped."

From a rear pocket, she withdrew a piece of paper and unfolded it. "This here is the wanted sign I was going to put up at the convenience store. Something you can do?"

Carpenter/Construction

Work Exchanged for Room & Board

Remodel and Upgrading

Basic Handyman Duties

The gods were shining down on him. How did he walk into the situation he most fit perfectly? If she wanted someone with an accounting background, he'd be out of luck. A chef? Forget it. But construction?

"Sounds perfect." He picked up his backpack and slung it over one shoulder. "When does it start?"

Her eyes narrowed. He could tell she was weighing her options. "Right now, follow me. I'll show you the home, and you can let me know if you're up for the job."

Chapter Two

The newcomer had pissed Tala off right away, telling her how to hang the B&B's sign. What a way to start the business. She knew all the guys who worked construction in town, and they were being kept pretty busy with rebuilding the grounds and with Drew's assignments. She never expected to find an out-of-towner to do the job, and so quick, too.

It was kind of eerie how fast he came along, and on the same day her brother left. What were the odds?

As she opened the front door, she did her best to hide the broken hinge. Soon enough, he'd find out all the house's faults, but she didn't want to scare him away too fast.

"You can set your bag down in the foyer while we do the tour." She held out her hand. "I'm Tala."

His handshake was firm and his hand slightly rough. She imagined working construction and hiking took its toll.

"Yas Collins." His blue eyes drew her in, and the

corners crinkled up as if he found something humorous. "How big is this place?"

"Eight bedrooms, including mine. The downstairs has a large family room, kitchen with a dining area, and two rooms. The rest are upstairs."

He stopped to run his fingers along one crack in the entranceway, and she hoped he didn't inspect the long-term damage too closely. Kind of hard to miss.

"Follow me," she said.

He went to take a step forward and faltered. "Let me get these boots off first. I don't want to track mud through your house."

Her heart jumped at the consideration. *Brawn and brains?* Her inner wolf growled at her sudden attraction. Domesticated did it for her, eh? That and his fair looks. The blond hair and pale skin was in such a contrast to her Native American heritage.

Leaning against the wall, he unlaced one boot and yanked it off before settling it gently to the floor. Off came the other one. Exposed beneath was a pair of bright-red socks with black polka dots. She raised an eyebrow and met his gaze.

"Gift from my little sis."

Sweet and forgivable.

She shook off the goo-goo eyes and continued with the tour. First, they headed through the large shared room and kitchen with its bay window. She winced, watching him take in the boarded-over panes. He glanced at her.

"Some kids broke out the window, and I haven't had a chance to get it fixed." She didn't need to tell him it had been almost two years before, and they hadn't bothered because the way things were before, odds were someone would just as fast throw more stones.

Her father had gotten into some bad business, years past, and within the pack, memories ran deep. She didn't meet new shifters too often. A tightening in her lower belly spread, surging energy throughout her body. What would it be like to shift with him and run under the full moon?

And make love in the soft grasses. She couldn't keep the fantasy out of her mind. It had been too long since she was with a man of worth. She'd grown tired of the local boys, who never seemed to want to grow up and take responsibility. Something in Yas's blood called to her. But if he was "just visiting," maybe he'd be fun to play with and not get attached.

She hated being prisoner to her animal instincts. She preferred to be in control. But there were a few times a month she let go. His eyes widened. No way he could guess what she was thinking. Unless the scent of her desire gave it away.

Inside, the house was in worse shape than he'd expected. Cracked walls, busted-out glass, and scrapes marred the floor in the kitchen. Water from the previous night's storm seeped through the broken windows and holes in the roof. That was only the surface—what could be seen. Who knew what lay inside the walls or the plumbing? What had he gotten into?

Tala kept checking him out, and when he thought she wasn't looking, he was doing pretty much the same. Her body language tightened up the longer the tour lasted. Maybe staying here wouldn't be such a good idea after all. He could handle staying above the bar if they had any availability. Without even trying, Tala pushed all his buttons.

Her ass swayed in her cute denim overalls as she climbed up the stairs, and his cock grew harder with each step. He counted the beats—step, sway to the right, step, sway to the left. Repeat. He'd been having trouble controlling his shifting, especially when turned on. He wanted to reach up, lay his hands on her hips, and feel the movement. His wolf liked what it saw.

What if she had another lover who visited her at the house? Would he lie in bed awake at night, listening to them pound the headboard into the wall?

A growl from low in his throat threatened to escape. The rumble started in his chest, and he fought to keep it down.

She turned, looking down at him. "Did you say something?"

"Umm, no. Just clearing my throat."

He needed to get his base instincts under control. Recent research showed that wolves in the wild killed in order to protect their domains and to get more space. He didn't want to be ruled by his wolf. He'd grown up in the city, with humans, not out in the forest. His mom had tried to talk to him about shifting, but as a woman, she didn't have the same experience.

He couldn't go to a shifters anonymous group for help with his sexual urges. Maybe he needed to start his own support group. He snorted at the idea. At the top of the landing, Tala turned to the right, and he followed.

They entered what had to be the master bedroom suite. It was painted a vibrant lavender color, and the bed had a green floral comforter with an abundance of fluffy throw pillows. White dollies rested on the two nightstands, and a vase of wildflowers called for attention. The feminine room seemed in sharp contrast to his host. She didn't look frilly.

"This will be your quarters." Her lips pursed, and she blinked a few times.

The idea shocked him. "What? I'm sorry, but it looks like your room."

"Well, it has been. But it's the nicest room in the house, and as a guest, figure you should have it to be comfortable. I'll move my things into another one."

He waved his hands in front of him, as if shooing away something physically bad. "No way. No can do. Give me the second best, then. My first job can be fixing it up."

She smiled. "Well, second best would be my brother's room, and even though he's on a trip right now, I don't feel comfortable moving his stuff. So third best, and we work today to make it more, um, livable?"

Her choice of words made him pause. "Deal."

As they walked down the hallway, things got worse. A whistling rattled, and he swore the floor shook. With all the doors shut, he wasn't sure where they were headed.

"This here is the bathroom." Tala pushed open a door.

He peeked in, taking in stains on the ceiling, which must have come from a bad leaky roof. By the looks of things, it had been in poor shape for a while.

Didn't her brother do any upkeep?

"And your room is the next on the left." She removed a key ring from her pocket and unlocked the door. "Safety reasons," she mumbled under her breath.

Once he stepped inside, he could see why. A gaping hole where a window should have been looked out onto the forest. Two birds rushed past them and outside. He looked up to the corner where they'd come.

"Is that a nest up there?"

"Probably. Better than bats, though, right?"

He shuddered. "I'm sorry, but I have to ask. Why didn't you board up that window?"

"Well, then the birds couldn't get to their nest, could they?"

The reasoning almost made sense to him. Except he'd be the one staying in the room. "Any other creatures I need to worry about?"

"Maybe a squirrel or two, depending upon the time of year."

"I see. Well." He surveyed the room. It really

was a quite stunning view, one he didn't get living in the city. The bed was stripped, and the mattress looked a bit worse for wear. "This room may take longer than this afternoon to become habitable."

He preferred not to share his space with wildlife, especially ones he may eat come shifting time. Unless, that is, he was living outdoors. Being in a home should have some basic comforts. This room was the best of the rest? He had his work cut out. He'd seen the oversize sectional downstairs. "Is the couch comfortable?"

"Soft," she said, "but clean and comfortable. I take naps there often."

He imagined her scent filling his nose as he drifted off to sleep. The thought aroused him once again. Maybe the plumbing didn't matter too much. He predicted an awful lot of cold showers in his future.

"Sold."

Chapter Three

The scent of roasting meat filled the house. Yas reached the kitchen and took in the beauty of Tala. The late-afternoon sunlight streamed in through the window—what was there—bathing her in hues of soft yellow and orange. Her long black hair flowed down her back, and she'd changed into a summery dress that stopped right at her knees, showing off her shapely calves.

She hummed a song he couldn't quite place.

"It smells good."

She jumped and dropped the wooden spoon. "Oh, you scared me. I'm not used to someone else being in the house. My brother clumped his feet so much I always knew he was coming."

As he bent to pick up the spoon, she reached down at the same time, and they clunked heads.

"Ouch, sorry," they said in unison.

"Jinx," she threw out, really fast.

He chuckled, holding out the spoon. "I owe you a

Co-Coke?" His mind had wanted to fill in "cock." He bit the side of his tongue, reining the beast in.

So she was beautiful, and from the smells, she knew how to cook. It didn't mean he needed to be aggressive. He'd take it easy, get to know her and the town. He hadn't come looking for a mate—not really—but as she turned to wash off the spoon, he took in the swish and sway of her hips and he needed to be reminded of the fact again.

Mate? Why was he even thinking that word? He was the handyman. That was all. *Handyman with benefits?* "Anything I can do to help?"

"I about have it covered. Did you get your things unpacked okay?"

"Mmmm-hmmm." He picked at the salad on the dining table. The crisp radish crunched in his mouth, and he savored the burst of freshness. For the time being, she'd given him a drawer in her room, and he'd only unloaded the essentials. He didn't travel with much.

Next to the stove, she stirred something and then put on some oven mitts to take out the roast.

"You didn't have to go through so much trouble." His stomach roared in protest. He wasn't too bad in the kitchen, but he rarely got a home-cooked meal. Everyone was too busy.

"Gives me practice for when this place is filled. It's a B&B, remember."

"Yes, but that second B usually stands for breakfast."

"Well, with how small our town is, I'll be a bit more full service."

Some plates and silverware sat on the counter, and he picked them up and laid them out at the table.

"You don't need to—"

"Hey, I'm happy to help." He had to keep his hands busy; otherwise, they'd get him in trouble.

A roast, potatoes, and vegetables—a bona fide feast in his eyes. All that was missing was the gravy, and then he caught Tala standing at the sink, pouring steaming gravy into a boat. His mouth watered. After the hike into the town and too many granola bars, real, hot food sounded too good.

They settled at the table. When she passed a

platter over to him, their fingers brushed, and he met her gaze. A slow smile spread across her face.

"I'm thankful you showed up today. I thought I'd be eating leftovers alone. It's good to have someone else here, to care for…."

"How long have you been alone?" he asked.

"Oh, not too long. My brother headed into the city to go to college. He was tired of being caged in a small town. Greener pastures, and all that. What brings you here to Los Lobos?"

"Greener pastures," he joked. "After growing up in the 'cement jungle,' I wanted to see where my mom came from, our roots. How about you? No desire to see the rest of the world?"

Tala finished chewing, glanced at the familiar knickknacks decorating the dining nook, and finally shrugged. "It may not be much, but this is my home. Some people are destined for more, have bigger dreams. Me? Maybe I'm stubborn or something. I can't imagine living anywhere else. Sometimes it might make my life easier though."

Although he understood where she was coming

from, the last statement was a bit curious.

"Easier how?"

"Let's enjoy the meal. We have plenty of time to talk. Sometimes a small town feels small."

After dishes, Tala said good night and slipped upstairs. She didn't normally go to bed so early, but being with Yas put her on edge. It was more than meeting someone new. She found him attractive—too much so. As a she-wolf, she was coming into her time. Shifting and sex often went together. With her brother in the house, she hadn't felt too comfortable running wild. With him gone, her hormones shifted into overdrive, and tonight the fantasies consisted entirely of her first houseguest, Yas.

She'd better stock up on sunscreen because with that fair skin and blond hair, he'd burn his first full day out in the sun. The city-boy wouldn't know what hit him. Mentally, she reviewed the list of supplies they'd have to pick up to get started, all the lumber and pipe. Plenty of people had seen him come through earlier in the day, and they were probably wondering where he'd gone. She'd have him review the list and see if she'd missed anything.

Where he slept in the living room lay directly underneath her bed. He'd probably taken his shirt off and was lounging down there now. She swallowed the surge of lust. A squeak outside her door made her jump.

"Night, Tala. I'm headed down to bed."

"Pleasant dreams," she managed to reply. Of course, he'd had to come upstairs to get ready. Before she drifted off, she prayed none of the vandals who'd been harassing her would come overnight. She didn't want to scare off Yas too soon.

The scent of the woman filled his nostrils. His body ached for release. She lay upstairs, so close to him, and yet the chasm between them was too great. Pain radiated along his legs, from his calves to upper thighs. He groaned as a white-hot lash struck across his shoulders, making him double over on the couch. Twisting and turning, he tumbled to the floor, knocking over a lamp.

Unforgiving wood offered no comfort to the heat pounding through his veins. He fought against the change. He needed to be in control, not his wolf.

"Are you all right down there?" Tala called.

Her lean silhouette stood at the top of the stairs. Light shone through her gown, and her luscious curves called to him. She took a step down.

"I'm fine." He gritted his teeth against the pain. "Just rolled off the couch."

The sound of footsteps came halfway down. "Can I get you anything? Do you need any help?"

"No. Don't." Spasms streaked across his shoulders again, and he growled. "Stay. Away."

Quicker, Tala rounded the corner of the living room and stopped. "Yas? What's wrong?"

His face morphed, shifting into a partial form. He opened his jaw, snapping at empty air, unable to vocalize what he wanted to say. A scream of frustration broke through, and he seized upon his humanity.

"I can't. Control. It. Get away."

Did she ever listen?

"I can help you, Yas."

Closer. He smelled her. The heat between her legs. He wanted to tear her clothes off. Bury his snout into her breasts. Lick her pussy. *Take her. Take her. Take her.*

The thought. Only that thought. Sliding his cock into her warmth. *Take her.*

With everything he possessed, he pushed off the hardwood floor and away from her. She followed, hand outstretched. Didn't she get it? She should fear him. Rocking, he sat on his heels, ready to jump at any movement.

Light fingers stroked the back of his neck, feathering through his hair. He tilted his head toward her touch and sighed. She was an angel, caressing away his doubts. Her stroke tamed his wolf. For a few moments, he considered she might be right. She could help him. All his wolf wanted was a little bit of attention and to meet the bearer of the scent firsthand.

Then she moved closer, her bare legs resting against his skin, and the wolf took over. He snaked his arm behind her knees, catching her off balance, and knocking her onto the couch. She exhaled with a loud "oomph" as she fell.

He pounced, straddling her. His cock nestled between her legs, pushing against the soft cotton of her underwear. Her mouth opened in a surprised O. Fuck foreplay or first kiss. His wolf wanted to sink deep inside her. *Now. In bocca al lupo*. Good luck with that.

"Well that was a bit unexpected." Her eyes sparkled in the dim lighting. Her musky scent grew stronger. She was turned on. She wanted him. Probably as much as he did her.

See? His wolf howled.

"Does this mean you're attracted to me, or do you greet all women in this manner in the middle of the night?"

Leaning over, he caught a whiff of her natural scent, and he sniffed her neck, from right below her ear all the way down her cleavage.

Tala shuffled beneath him, trying to break free. "Dude, watch the sniffing. It's a bit creepy. While I've enjoyed our little interaction, anything more is a bit too soon for me, understand? I just met you today."

His wolf didn't care. From first sight, he knew he'd have her. He lusted after her.

She banged her fist against his arm. "Did you hear me? Get off. Let me up."

A battle for control warred within his body. The duality tore him apart. He should have known better than to think he could control it. He snarled, baring his teeth, and threw his body to the side. He rolled onto the floor.

With a fluid movement, Tala took to her feet. She brushed off her nightgown and fisted her hands on her hips. "You are quite a handful, aren't you?"

Weak from the internal fight, he lay on the floor, willing her to leave him be. Without her presence, he'd tame the beast.

"I know what makes me feel better. A good run."

With those words, she stripped off her nightgown and stood before him nude. On fire, his body roared as he shifted into his wolf form.

She whistled. "Look at you. You're gorgeous.

Your fur is so blond, it looks white…like the snow."

After opening the front door, she stood basking in the moonlight streaming in. He advanced, and, in a blink of his eyes, she'd shifted into a wolf. She opened her mouth in a grin and bounded outside. He followed.

Cool night air clung to Yas's fur as he pounded through the woods. His heart raced with the speed of his body. Every now and then he caught a glimpse of Tala running in front of him. But she remained out of reach. She ran with a sure comfortableness in her own backwoods.

Freedom. Running in parks at home had nothing on this experience. The moon guided them in its warm embrace. With each passing moment, the built-up fury within his body dissipated. She led him to a small river, and they stopped to get a soothing drink of water. She stood just far enough away that if he advanced, she could get away. At the moment, he didn't care.

Fresh green earth and dirt. He dug his nose into the ground and pawed at the long grasses. Tala yipped at him, capturing his attention. With a swish of her tail, she took off again in the direction of the house. As her sight diminished, Yas stretched out in the clearing and stared up into the open sky. Power from Mother Nature surged within his body, and he wished he could better control some of the aspects of shifting.

When he started changing into his wolf form, he'd thought of it as a curse. Now, lying in the forest with the open world surrounding him, for the first time he believed it might instead be a blessing.

Chapter Four

Working construction on and off for the last five years, Yas naturally woke up early. After making a pot of coffee, he went out to the front porch with a pad of paper and pen. With one hand on the top of a chair, he tested its sturdiness. It seemed stable enough. The old wood groaned under his weight, but it held together. Since it's what potential customers saw first, it needed to go on top of the list. He could sand down the wood, repair some missing pieces, and repaint it, probably in a day. Two at the most.

Inside? He shook his head as he made notes for the breakfast nook and upstairs bedrooms. He suspected the home needed more repairs than Tala was letting him see at the moment. Pride probably kept her from allowing him to get too close of a look, especially at her room.

Dew glistened on the grass as the sun took hold more overhead. A few birds called to each other, rejoicing another night survived, and another day to live. He shut his eyes, breathing in the fresh air and letting his mind wander. After he settled down, he hoped to send word to his little sister.

Sugar wouldn't care to be called "little" much. The last time he'd seen her, she'd planned on rushing a sorority. He had a hard time imagining Little Miss Prissy in the wild of Los Lobos, but the lack of concrete jungle would do her well.

The front door opened with a creak, and the scent of baking blueberries drifted out with Tala.

"You're up early," she said, leaning against the jamb. She wore a soft-yellow robe that reflected the early morning light and cast her in a glowing halo.

He shielded his eyes to meet her gaze directly. "Habit. Something smells good."

Her smile increased the glow. "Blueberry scones. Hungry?"

"You don't need to do anything fancy for me."

"Who says they're for you? If you're going to get this place up and running fast, then I better get used to serving the guests."

"Expecting an influx of newcomers to the area?"

She gazed out over the yard and the rooftops of the main town area in the distance. "We've already seen some new faces since Magnum died and his son Drew took over. With all the remodeling and improvements, I'm sure our little community will expand. Not that we're advertising for new settlers or anything. We like to keep it private."

"Probably not." He stood, stretching out. Maybe one of the rooms should be higher on that list. The couch wasn't the most comfortable spot to crash. "While we eat, let's go over the supply list, and tell me what you think. Any tools you think we might need, or already have?"

With a nod, she took the paper from him. Their hands touched, and he swore the feeling traveled all the way from his fingertips, through his body, and straight to his cock.

Even with doing his best to suppress the urges, it didn't work. Maybe he wasn't meant to be around others. He thought being out in the wild would be better for him, but living under the same roof as Tala wasn't helping.

After breakfast, they set out on a trip to Los Lobos Lumber. Tala knew there would be a lot of questions about her brother leaving, and, hopefully, the introduction of a newcomer would prove to be a distraction.

"What type of tools do you have at the house?" Yas asked. Already, he'd been surprised that she didn't own some sort of vehicle. How would she get by without a truck out here? The lumberyard would deliver when needed.

"My brother had the basics—hammer, screwdrivers. But if you're looking for fancy saws, you'll have to rent those."

Her handyman nodded, but his expression looked anything but pleased. She only hoped whatever negative sentiment had targeted their house didn't extend to Ogden, the owner of the lumberyard.

Their feet kicked up dirt as they walked, and the silence grated on Tala's nerves. "How old were you when you first shifted?" she asked. Might as well talk while they walked.

Tense muscles constricted on Yas's body. "Late teens."

Well, that gave her a lot of information. Every Wolf was different, every shift different. A late bloomer, as it were, might have more issues. "Anyone tell you what to expect?"

His jaw muscles flexed, and he gritted his teeth. "Ma put off getting into specifics about it. Once it happened…well, I learned."

Again, the sound of their footsteps overpowered just about everything else. Tala listened to her blood pulsing through her head. She counted the rhythms before trying again. "How about your sister, does she…?"

He stopped. "Do you want to get all your questions out now? Because I'm trying to lay out what needs to be done at your house, and you keep interrupting my train of thought."

What crawled up his tail this morning? With a huff, she kept walking, refusing to look behind to see if he followed. Eventually, he would. She rounded a corner. Up ahead, five teenagers played kickball in the street, blocking the road. She tensed, expecting the worst from boys that age. Hormones.

A whistle, shrill and drawn out, cut through the air.

"Well, look at what we have here," the tallest called out, lifting his nose and catching her scent. "What's a pretty shifter like you doing out?"

The mini-pack spread apart, instinctively fanning out, as if to circle her. The best thing to do would be to stand her ground and not show any fear. And hope Yas hurried the hell up.

"Afternoon." She made eye contact with each of them, trying not to cringe under their leers. She looked younger than her twenty-four years.

The ringleader moved closer, his nostrils flaring. "I hear your brother headed out and left you all alone."

She didn't recognize the kid and had no idea how he knew her business. Small town, though, everyone knew everything—fast.

He took a step and in her peripheral vision, she

saw another teen move behind her, cutting off the escape route. Where the hell was Yas? These kids had no right making her feel unsafe.

"I'm headed to the lumberyard if you don't mind." She sidestepped, taking a move to cut around him. He mirrored her actions, blocking the way.

"What's your hurry? They're open for a long time still." He reached out, moving his hand toward her hair.

Dodging, she swung out to block his arm. "Don't touch me."

He laughed, low and mean. "Don't insult me." Quick, he grabbed at her arm, clutching the upper portion tight enough to hurt.

She jerked, without any give. One of the other boys in the pack hollered. The sound reminded her of a hunting party, and she shivered. They were teenagers. They should know better. With everything out of control in Los Lobos, some things slipped between the cracks.

"Who will protect you?" Her brother's words resurfaced to haunt Tala.

A growl shattered the laughter.

"Get your fucking hand off her."

Yas managed to sneak up on all of them, and an uncertain look surfaced in the closest teen's eyes. Yas weighed the situation. He could definitely take a few of them, and the others would run. Once the leader went down, the rest would fall. While the kid was already big for his age, Yas was much bigger, and an unknown. A stranger.

"Hey," Tala said. "Glad you caught up."

"That didn't take you long did it?" the teen said. "Your brother leaves and already you have another Wolf in the house?"

"How the hell did you guess that?" Yas moved in. If the kid didn't retreat, he'd make him.

"Clemet, she's not worth it." A scrawny boy who looked about fifteen tugged on his friend's shirt.

I have to file away that name for the future.

"I wouldn't say that," the ringleader replied. He leaned in close to Tala and made a show of inhaling loudly. "She smells like you."

He shoved Tala at Yas, who gracefully caught her, and moved her behind him in a safety position.

"You will leave her alone," Yas confronted the teen.

The boy's mouth turned up in a snarl. He didn't like being told what to do. He probably didn't have a father at home. *I know that feeling.*

Clemet held up his hands, as if making peace. "Hey, it's all good. We were just saying hello, isn't that true Tala?" He stroked her name over his tongue in a manner that put Yas on edge.

Gripping his fists until his nails cut into his palms, Yas addressed the situation again. "Get out of here, and I don't want to hear of you giving Ms. Graystone any more trouble. Do you hear me?"

"Perfectly clear, old man. Does that mean you'll be sticking around to watch over her?"

The implied threat hung in the air, and the hairs on Yas's neck stood up. He fought his Wolf. He didn't want to shift. Right now, it would just get him into trouble. Controlling his temper in human form was bad enough. As a Wolf? He may tear these kids to shreds. They were assholes, but they didn't deserve that.

The skin along his forehead rippled, and Clemet's gaze drifted up before his pupils grew wider, and he knocked his friend in the shoulder. "Let's get out of here."

In unison, they moved to leave. They'd obviously been together, carving out their own pecking order.

All soft curves, Tala embraced him. Such a contrast to his tense muscles. The feeling of her body against his ratcheted his desire higher. He wanted her. If he couldn't kick the shit out of someone—and that someone now retreated—then he wanted to fuck someone. All this extra adrenaline and nowhere to put it, nothing to do with it. He needed to break free. Instead, he did what he could to taper it down.

"My hero," she said in a soft tone. Her body shook. "Thanks for saving me. How can I possibly thank you?"

"It was nothing, ma'am." Yas affected a country-western drawl.

"Hey, Tala." From the top of the ridge, Clemet

43

called out. "How's that kitchen bay window doing? Sure lets in some beautiful light in the morning. Kinda drafty though."

In his arms, Tala stilled and turned toward the laughing teens. They were far enough away that if he chased after them, they had a good head start. But not too far that he couldn't catch 'em.

"Notice how they sound more like hyenas than wolves?" she said against his chest. "Just let them go. I don't want any more trouble."

"If that's what you want." She might not have gotten it, but the "more" in her request clued him in that more had been happening then she'd let on. If that was the case, how could her brother have left her all alone?

Up ahead was Los Lobos Lumber. The smell of freshly cut wood caused a bit of a homecoming for Yas. For as long as he could remember, he'd liked crafting stuff with his hands, the art of making something out of nothing. An empty field replaced by a home, filled with a family and love. Idealistic for a construction worker? Maybe, but he was more of a craftsman.

"Hey there, how can I help you?" a tanned man, who probably spent a lot of time in the sun working, greeted them.

"Afternoon, Ogden," Tala said, "how's Lara doing?"

"Just fine. Thanks for asking. I didn't expect to see you so soon after your brother left." He shifted his gaze over to Yas before glancing at Tala.

"Yeah, well, just because he left doesn't mean my plans for the house went with him. This here is Yas. He happened to come along at the right time. Ogden owns the lumberyard."

That was his cue to hold out his hand to shake. The other man gripped his hand firmly and looked him directly in the eyes. At first glance, Yas might take him for being a bit more relaxed with his silver-streaked temples and easy smile, but something told him he should not underestimate Ogden.

"Good to meet you," the man said. "What can I help you with today?"

While Yas handed over the list of supplies to

purchase and items he hoped to borrow, he divided his attention to the others in the vicinity. Tala attracted attention. Being out with him, a stranger, probably added to the curiosity factor. As they moved through the yard, checking out the stock, he caught hidden glimpses and outright stares.

"With all this stuff, do you plan on adding on a third floor or something?" Ogden let out a low whistle.

"Not much has been done," Tala said. "The house needs a major overhaul before I can start bringing in other guests."

Ogden made eye contact with Yas, as if to receive a visual confirmation. "Sad but true. It gives me a place to stay for a while and a way to keep busy."

"What's your background in building?"

"I worked pretty regular jobs for the last five years. Started in elementary school with woodworking. Growing up with a single mother and sister, anything went wrong in the house, the repair usually fell to me."

The owner nodded his approval and made some figures on the sheet. He handed it over to Tala, and ever so slightly her eyes widened.

"It's a bit higher than I expected," she said.

"That's a good deal. With all the construction happening, supplies are getting scarce. Sure, we've got the forest, but getting the raw material into shape to build with takes time. And we only have so big of a workforce."

Yas peered over her shoulder to check out the figure. It didn't seem unreasonable. Much less than on the outside world. "When can you deliver?"

Tala inhaled as if to protest and then thought better of it. What was the alternative? Her cutting the trees and prepping them for building?

"Tomorrow."

***

After paying a deposit, they returned home without incident. Tala lifted the edge of the curtain and watched Yas sand the deck. At the moment, he was down on hands and knees, giving her a perfect view of his ass in his tight jeans. In the late-afternoon heat, he'd stripped off his shirt and his back glistened. The musculature along his arms tempted her to go out there and offer to help—just to be close to him.

His skin would taste salty, and she imagined herself as the reason for his exertion—his strong body raised over hers while he ravaged her. She pushed her hair from her face and let the curtain fall. Look at her all horny. No escaping she found him attractive. Hell, she wanted to jump him. It had been too long since she'd been with a lover. Living under the same roof as a protective older brother tended to squash her sex life. As a shifter, he should understand the carnal urges. That probably was the problem. Her brother understood too well and had kept her libido locked up.

Now that he was gone, though, she possessed the freedom to do what—and who—she chose. Some type of decision made, she headed to the kitchen. If he was so hot out there, he'd be thirsty. She'd make a refreshing glass of lemonade to pick him up.

Before heading out, Tala brushed out her hair and

put on some lip gloss. Since she'd been working inside, she didn't want to look too put together. Still, she wanted him to notice her.

The front door creaked as she opened it, and Yas looked in her direction. His gaze zeroed in on the glass in her hand, and he sat on his heels.

"I'm hoping that's for me," he said with a smile that did all sorts of things to her heart.

"Thought you might need to cool off." She walked closer to him and couldn't help but catch how he checked her out, starting at her feet then sliding up her bare legs and over her body. She handed him the drink, and his fingers brushed against hers.

"Thanks for thinking of me."

If he only knew.

"How's it going out here?" She surveyed the work he'd done so far.

"Faster than I thought. When you work on a project, it can be easy or slow. With a newer covering, it might take longer to remove. This paint's so old, it's coming off like dust."

The speckles on his arms and face reinforced his

statement, and she stifled a laugh. "I can see that. Have you been frolicking through all that 'dust'?"

"What?" He checked out his spotted arms. "Just what I need, to be even whiter than I already am. It should all come off in the shower."

"Mmmm-hmmm, and you better get cleaned up first thing. I don't want all that getting in the house."

"Yes, ma'am." He saluted and took a long draw of lemonade. His mouth puckered up, and his eyes crossed. "Wow. Sour."

"I hope you're exaggerating. It's better than being too sweet."

"Here, taste." He stood, took another sip, and then pulled her tight to his body. The heat radiated off his skin, and he pressed his cool lips against hers.

Shocked by his actions, Tala didn't react. She took in all the elements. The feel of his body. The enticing scent coming off his skin, appropriately like smoldering wood. Soon, she grew more aware of the weight of Yas's arm on her waist and the insistence of his kiss.

She parted her mouth, tentatively touching her

tongue along his bottom lip. He tasted tangy and refreshing. He deepened the kiss, drawing out her tongue, until they breathed the same air.

Everything changed with this one liplock. It was as if she'd never been kissed before, and never would feel this same way again. He, they, this moment became the center of her being. Everything else fell away.

The air between them made her realize the kiss had ended.

"So?" he asked, prodding her with more than his words.

She opened her eyes, recognizing a bit of mirth in his.

"How does it taste?"

She smacked her lips together. "Exactly how I like it."

Chapter Five

Soft tendrils of her hair brushed across his face, and he breathed in her scent. The fine lines at the corner of her eyes crinkled and smoothed as they widened. She glanced down at his lips, and he knew they both wanted more.

Yas wove his arm around her back, relishing the surprised "oh" escaping from her mouth and the slight parting of her lips. Her breath brushed his lips. The curves of her body pressed against the hard planes of his. *To feel her naked. To take her.* His desire raged, and he tamped it down. First, this step and then maybe….

Before he could internally argue further, she took the choice away. She moved closer, placed her leg between his and her lips on his. His blood surged, and his Wolf wanted to run wild and rip off all her clothes. What the hell was he thinking?

He wasn't.

Pure pleasure ripped through his body. The tip of

Tala's tongue lashed his lower lip, stroking, and Yas delved in. She tasted of honey, sweet with a hint of underlying spice. He tunneled his fingers into her hair, tugging slightly and holding her in place. She moaned against his mouth, encouraging him, enticing him.

The loss of control scared the hell out of him. He dropped his arms and stepped away, breaking the physical connection.

"What was that for?" She held the fingertips of one hand to her lips.

The memory of her kiss continued to tingle. "I've been thinking of kissing that sassy mouth of yours for days now," Yas said. "Figured if I did, maybe I'd get it out of my system."

"Did it work?"

"Nope. Only want more."

Shivers of anticipation alerted his body. When she didn't respond further, he cleared his throat. He didn't want to push it too much. "Thanks for the refreshment. Did you need me for anything else?"

"Want to check out the competition?" Tala's

question piqued his interest.

They hadn't talked as much while they worked. So far that morning, she'd avoided him, or at least that was how Yas had interpreted her distance.

"What competition would you be talking about?" He wiped the sweat from his brow, rested his hands on his waist, and stretched out his tense muscles.

"Gee's Bar. Along with grub and beer, he rents out rooms on the second floor. Up until now, it's the only business for lodging."

On the way into town, he'd passed the bar. Right then, he was damn thankful he'd kept on until reaching this place. "You don't think he has anything to do with what's been happening here, do you? Would he feel threatened by you?"

Lightness brightened her eyes, along with a smile. A pang in his heart mirrored the twitching of his cock. *Can I please get the physical responses under control?*

"Aww, Gee's just a cuddly old bear. He wouldn't hurt anyone, unless they threatened those he loves. No, just thought it would be good to investigate what he's offering specifically in comparison to my B&B."

Interesting choice of words. "Sure, what time you want to head out?"

"I was thinking dinnertime. This way we can get out the evening crowd and grab supper at the same time."

He did the mental math of the rest of the project that needed to be finished and pushed it off. "I'll be ready."

With a nod, Tala went into the house, and Yas picked up the hammer to patch the wall.

***

At the appointed time, Yas showered, dressed, and waited for his dinner date in the living room. A creak on the stairs alerted him to Tala's approach. She stepped into the foyer, and the light streaming in from the fixed window gave her hair shimmer.

Dude, get yourself under control. You don't have plans to stay here. Remember, this was only supposed to be a quick trip to discover your roots. You're already too involved.

He cocked his elbow, and she placed her hand on the crook. As they stepped outside, she locked the door.

"It's been a long time since that worked properly," she said. "I swear, some days it refused to lock at all. That's why I started to use the chains on the inside. Other days, it boycotted opening." She squeezed his arm in jest. "Are you tired of me thanking you yet?"

"Honey, I don't think I could ever grow tired of you."

They walked the road to Gee's Bar. As they grew near, the titter of laughter and glasses clinking resounded from inside. As they stepped near the entrance, Tala gave him a strained smile. She crinkled her eyes, as if worried about something she'd forgotten or pushed aside.

"Are you ready?"

"Sure, why wouldn't I be?"

The moment they stepped in, chatter halted and the collective gaze of all the inhabitants turned toward them. *Maybe not.*

"Hey there, Paul," she greeted the waiter. "Should we sit anywhere in particular?"

The man swept his arm out in front of him, gesturing toward some open tables.

"Gotcha. I'll fill my guest in on the menu."

With a nod, the waiter walked over to another table and bused the plates.

"He doesn't talk," Tala said, leading the way. "Rumor has it Magnum cut out his tongue."

With a shudder, Yas pressed his tongue to the roof of his mouth. He'd never really thought about it, but how did one talk without the appendage?

They didn't.

"I'm starving," he said. "You keep me pretty busy. I need lots of calories while I'm working, especially in the heat."

"Oh, poor baby. Here's the menu."

She handed him a small piece of paper about the size of a notecard. On it were written three items: fried pickles, hamburger, and steamed broccoli. He noticed a little hand-drawn star with a corresponding legend along the bottom.

**Cheese when in season

A laugh burst from his gut. When was the "season" for cheese?

He flipped the menu over, not sure whether he was hoping or not hoping for something on the other side.

"There's nothing there," Tala said. "Limited menu."

"I got that. Makes the selection easy. I think I'll have the hamburger. Want to split fried pickles?"

"Can't ever come here without 'em. Or you know, we could order the pickles with a side of hamburger."

He liked how she played along. The waiter dropped off two mugs of frosty beer. So far, they hadn't ordered anything, but Yas never turned away an icy beer, especially at the end of a long workday. He raised his eyebrow in question at Tala.

"We do things a bit differently here," she explained, before placing an order for two "specials" with Paul.

A loud guffaw from behind the bar drew his

attention. It was a man—the tallest he'd seen not on television—and packed with pure muscle. As he laughed, he pounded the wood bar and all the glasses shook.

Tala followed his line of sight. "That's Gee, the owner."

"Wouldn't want to be accused of doing him wrong." Yas took a gulp of his beer and sputtered, spewing ale over the table and his shirt. He inhaled some of the liquid, and it went down the wrong pipe.

Tala leaned over and whapped him until he held his hand up in defeat.

"I'm good," he choked out. "Don't hit me anymore."

The atmosphere in the bar shifted, and the hairs on the back of Yas's neck prickled. He turned to see Gee making his way through the crowd in a straight beeline for them.

"Get ready for the introduction," Tala warned.

"Tala," Gee said in a deep, resonating voice. "It's good to see you out."

"I'm happy to be out. I hate to miss Sundays at

your place."

Niceties over, all his attention shifted to Yas. "How's Sugar doing?"

Senses on full alert, he studied the bear of a man. "What? How do you know Sugar?"

"You are Janae's son, right?" he said in a matter-of-fact tone. "Of course I remember your sister. She was just a wee little thing."

Music started up all at once, causing Yas to jump. The world spun, and yet time stretched and he felt frozen at this moment. When he came to Los Lobos, he'd expected to hunt for information, or maybe find nothing at all. He never thought someone would recognize him, and know his history. And yet here he was.

"Don't mind Gee. He knows everyone." Tala placed her hand on his forearm, acting as a centering point.

He fought the urge to shrug her off. Nothing was her fault. Why was he getting so worked up? "What can you tell me about our time here, or my father?"

The waiter appeared, setting the plates in front of

them. Steam wafted up, and Yas reclined, antsy at the distraction.

The bar's owner met his gaze. "Only that you've come here at the right time." He flicked his eyes toward Tala and then back to Yas. "Enjoy your meal."

With those parting words, Gee made his rounds of the restaurant. Yas scooted his chair as if to follow him, and Tala shook her head.

"That was downright chatty for Gee. Unless it's his idea to share some knowledge with you, you're not getting it." She picked up a fried pickle and popped it in her mouth, smiling at the crunch. "At least now I can rest assured that you were telling me the truth about being from here."

"Really? You doubted me, and still you let me move into your home?"

"Well, I'm awfully good with a shotgun."

Her outlandish statement threw him. Sure, they lived out in the wild, away from much traditional civilization, but weapons?

"What do you need to protect yourself from?"

She batted her eyes. "These parts have settled down an awful lot in the past few years, but there are still those who cannot fully be trusted, and we have some warring neighbors. Just being safe."

He picked up his burger, juice dripping down the sides of his hands, and sank his teeth into it. A moan escaped his mouth. He couldn't remember ever tasting simple meat so good. It was the perfect combination of cooked but not dry. No one would be calling the health department here after getting ill on "raw" meat. "This is fantastic."

"That's how they get away with such a limited menu. What else do you need?"

They consumed dinner in silence. The head on the beer tickled his nose as he took a long gulp.

"I might not be able to walk home. You might have to roll me," he said.

Tala laughed. He noticed a speck of ketchup at the edge of her lip, and he reached over to wipe it with his napkin. She stopped, her eyes darkening. The sexual desire between them heightened, and he swore everyone in the bar could feel it.

He swallowed. Unless he wanted to jump her right here, he better go with distraction. "We should have asked Gee about seeing upstairs while we had him."

"We don't really have to check out the rooms. Just eating here, I figured you'd get a feel for this place."

"How quiet are the bedrooms? With all this action happening down below, I'd think the sound would travel. The acoustics."

"I've never stayed here myself, and it's popular. Can't really say."

Yas pondered the situation. Obviously, there was quite the contrast between Gee's Bar, in the heart of everything, and Tala's B&B. It would be in her best interest to heighten those points. Cater to the more quiet and laid-back atmosphere. Paul placed the bill on the table, and Tala grabbed it.

"You're working at my place. Let me pick up dinner. I'm sure I'll get every bite in return." She played with her bottom lip between her teeth, and a wicked sparkle in her eye told him she was teasing.

63

Despite mentioning how full he was a few minutes ago, a new hunger overtook him. What would it be like knowing they were returning home as a couple? That he could have his way with her at will, whenever he wanted?

That he had a home? A sense of longing overcame him. Yes, his mom did the best she could, but still he searched for that one special place he belonged. He never connected with it in college or any other bigger cities he'd lived in. Not until he'd arrived here and met Tala that his wolf spirit grew quiet.

Now to tame his sexual urges.

***

On the way to the house, Yas grew quiet and pensive. What could he be thinking about? Gee probably threw him for a loop. Maybe she should have warned him beforehand. He was their version of Yoda from *Star Wars*—yes, she'd seen the original films—he only shared what he wanted. Most often, that didn't line up with what the other person wanted

64

to hear.

Being with Yas last night had shifted their relationship. She couldn't be near him without thinking of being with him. With her brother just leaving, she wasn't in a position where she wanted to get into a relationship, but maybe things could work out with Yas. His plans were to only stay for a few weeks and then move on. While her heart knew it was dangerous territory, she considered having a physical relationship with him.

A handyman with benefits?

She snickered and caught Yas looking at her from the side.

"What's so funny?" he asked.

"Oh, just thinking. You know how it is. Walking, and if it gets quiet, the mind tends to wander."

His grunt acknowledged her explanation, but he didn't push further. Once they'd started to talk, she continued.

"Thanks for going with me to Gee's. Get any ideas?"

Stopping, he shoved his hands into his pockets

and turned to gaze toward the lights of the town. "A few. It was more interesting learning about the people of the town more. Is everyone a shifter?"

"Not everyone. Recently, we've had a few humans join our ranks, and not everyone turns into a wolf either. I've seen others, heard tales."

He ran his hand through his hair. "I hadn't really thought of it. It makes sense. Any territory issues?"

"Some, especially with the big-cat shifters. Canines and cats tend to not get along."

"Humpf," Yas grunted.

The darkness shifted as the moon rose higher and grew brighter. Together, they both glanced upward.

He took her hand. "Anything you should worry about? Anything I should worry about?"

All her senses flowed to their physical connection. She couldn't ignore the sexual tension between. Having him last night in the wild only increased her desire. "Not really," she said, focusing on the issue at hand and not the hormones raging in her body. "The damage on the house might be vandals or teen pranks." *Like those boys the other day*.

"Gone too far," Yas said. "Well, I'll make it my job to figure out who's the culprit and that you're safe before I leave."

Moving away from him, she guarded her face. *Another man to the rescue*. Right, she wanted his brawn for repairs. Well, and sex. She didn't need to be "protected."

Chapter Six

Yas may have good intentions, but alone with Tala everything changed. It was much easier to control his attraction for her while in a bar full of people. Once the door shut, the energy between them spiked.

She lay on the couch, head reclined, and eyes closed. The edge of her dress rose on her thigh, and he drank in the sight of her bare skin.

The hell with resistance. He moved with purpose, settling next to her. At the feel of his body, she opened her eyes and held his gaze. Understanding passed between them. There was no denying it. He wanted her more than anything else in his life. The small taste that afternoon did nothing to subdue the hunger.

"What's your pleasure?" Yas trailed his hand along the outside of Tala's thigh.

Her eyes widened, and the pupils expanded at the touch. They'd been coming to this moment, facing their attraction rather than avoiding it, for a while. The earlier kiss only added kindling to the fire.

She worried her lower lip between her teeth and studied his expression. She moved her hand to cover his, and he thought she'd still him, stop his movement. Instead, she directed him to her ass, sliding closer until their mouths were mere inches apart. Her breath caressed his lips.

Long, dark lashes fanned against her cheeks as she looked down. "You. You are my pleasure."

Desire flared as high as a fire with lighter fluid squirted on it with abandon. He'd expected a flame retardant. Instead, she provided an accelerant.

He bridged the remaining gap, taking in her soft, succulent lips. Hesitant at first, he ran the tip of his tongue along the top of her mouth, teasing, asking permission to enter. The slightest parting, and he was in. Tasting her inner warmth.

A soft moan against his mouth drew him in, and the hunger increased. His wolf growled low within his soul, wanting to come out to play. To take over his action.

One kiss, and his wolf wanted to fuck.

Things tended not to go too well when the wolf took over. Base emotions. No feelings. Pure physical sensation. Oh sure, Yas had to admit he didn't mind it all that much, but still…. He didn't want to hear complaints that he wasn't there, present, with her enough. He didn't want to check out as the wolf checked in.

This time, he wanted it to be different. He wanted to remain in control. His love interest. His woman. His fuck.

The wolf didn't like it. It felt sometimes as if he was two separate halves warring for occupation within his body.

"Hey, where did you go?" Delicate hands cupped his face, and Tala gazed at him all concerned. "You drifted off all of a sudden."

Point taken. "I'm sorry, maybe we shouldn't…."

Tala placed her hands against his chest, using his body for support, and straddled his lap. Her skirt flowed over him, and the sweet V of her thighs rubbed directly over his shaft. She looped her arms behind his neck. "What were you saying?"

"Uh, nothing." A case of the stupids struck.

She sucked on his bottom lip, and the sensations streaked through his entire body, concentrating in his cock.

"Someone sure likes this," she commented, grinding her pelvis against him. "And I like it an awful lot."

Gritting his teeth, he tempered his wolf. "Too much."

"It can never be too much."

They lost all sense of time and space, sinking into the feeling of connection. He pushed his hand under her shirt, cupping her full breast. With his thumb, he brushed against her nipple and smiled at her sharp intake of breath.

He'd been looking at these babies through her clothing, and now he wanted a firsthand peek. Lifting her shirt over her body, he drank in the swells of her breasts in her purple bra.

A loud whining sound broke the mood, and Yas retreated. "What the hell was that?"

Before Tala had a chance to answer, a knocking sounded on the door.

"That was the doorbell," Tala said, yanking her shirt down.

And there they go.

She stood, crossing the living room to the front door.

"Add that to the list of items to be fixed," he muttered.

Tala smoothed her hair and opened the door. The moment she saw who it was, she stepped closer, blocking the slight opening.

Curious, Yas drew closer. The entire time he'd been there, except for the delivery, they hadn't received any visitors. They. As if they were a *they*.

"Hey, Ryker. What can I do for you?"

A low baritone voice rumbled. Since the speaker was on the other side of the door, Yas couldn't quite hear what was being said. He noticed, though, the body language of the she-wolf who'd been in his arms moments ago. No longer relaxed. Every muscle tensed, as if she was ready to shift into fight-or-flight mode.

If he hadn't been watching, he wouldn't have noticed it, but ever so slightly she leaned back and glanced in his direction. Then he knew. They were talking about him.

"Hey, Tala," he said, "Is everything all right?"

This time, when she looked at him, her eyes flashed with anger. He was supposed to stay in the background like a good little wolf.

Fuck that shit, his wolf said for an altogether different reason.

He gripped the door, and she stepped out of the way, giving him one last warning look.

"Hi, can I help you with something?" he asked.

The man standing in front of his was tall with long dark hair. Almost as tall as Yas. His American Indian features told of a long history of living on the land. He emitted a sense of authority. He glanced at Yas's outstretched hand, and the side of his lip snarled upward.

"Ryker. I heard we had an interloper in town."

"Interloper?" Yas wanted to laugh at the archaic

vocabulary.

The men sized each other up.

"I don't expect any trouble from you," Ryker said.

Yas shoved his hands into his pockets. "I'm not planning on making any, but"—he glanced at Tala—"if someone comes at me, I'm not the type to run away with my tail between my legs."

Ryker accessed him. "Fair enough. How long were you planning on staying?"

Get right to the point, why don't you buddy.

"I figured a few weeks originally." He paused. "But Tala could use some help around here, and I don't have anything pressing happening. So for right now, let's say for as long as I'm needed."

With a final nod, the man turned and headed off. Yas stepped into the house and shut the door.

"What the hell was that all about?"

"Ryker is basically the 'law' around here," she explained. "He keeps the peace and also makes sure everyone stays in line. Often, he's behind the scenes. If you see him in an official capacity, it's usually not a good thing. Though, since he met up with his mate Saja, he's mellowed out a bit."

"If that's mellow, I'd hate to see him riled up," Yas said. "Now, where were we before he so rudely interrupted us?"

Her eyes widened as he moved toward her. With a sly smile, she tried to outmaneuver him, but for each step to the right or left, he kept pace.

"I think you're trying to catch me," she replied, before turning and dashing out the door.

Outside, the night was darker than any in the city, and mother moon had laid a streak of light in a path. Still in human form, Tala ran, and Yas's wolf urged him to run faster.

One following the other, they crested a small hill, and he closed the gap between. Racing downhill, the force of their speed took over, and they tumbled, rolling down the soft grass, landing with him on top of her. Yas wedged his knee between Tala's thighs. Her hair fanned in a halo around her head. She gazed up and him, and parted her lips ever so slightly.

The tension between them stretched out time.

Her chest heaved from the exertion of their running. He rested on his elbows and shifted his weight to one side. He stroked her hair, caressing the side of her face.

"You're so beautiful."

She bit her lip and looked to the side. Wetness slipped down her cheek. He brushed away the tears.

"Hey, what's up? Why so sad?

She took a deep breath, and the expansion of her stomach pressed against his body. "I want you, but I can't be with you."

His insides clenched. Would he be any good for her? He'd only known her for a short while and never planned to stay. Should he be selfish and be with her simply because he lusted after her?

"Why? I think we'd be good together."

"I see you, though. How you hold yourself back. I want someone who's willing to lose himself."

He fought against the instinct to push up and walk away. She was worth more than his normal reaction. For a long time, all of his emotions had been shut up. "That's not true. I do care."

Bringing his mouth flush against hers, he set about to prove he could be the wolf she needed. Staying in Los Lobos may not have been his original plan, but somewhere over the last two weeks, his priorities had shifted. Where else could he go to feel so welcomed and at home?

He'd come to this town looking for part of his past, and he'd found his future.

Tala stiffened beneath him, but as his tongue sought out hers, she softened. She may act all tough on the outside, but he knew she'd locked away a heart of gold on the inside. Why didn't others see that? He couldn't be the only one to discover her wealth.

She slipped one hand under his T-shirt, raking her nails across his sensitive skin. He moaned against her mouth.

So good. How could one person feel so incredibly right beneath his body? Her curves molded against him. He rose, breaking the connection. Her eyes sparkled with a wicked lust.

"Is that all you got?" she asked.

"Are you comfortable? Am I squashing you?"

"Has anyone ever told you that sometimes you can be too nice?" She hooked a foot over his calf. "You kiss better than I imagined."

"Well, I had some help there. Too nice? I'll show you too nice." *Hell, that's not what I usually hear. I've been having the opposite problem—taking things too far, too fast.*

Reaching between their bodies, he lifted her shirt over her head and took in the sight of her gorgeous breasts. He dipped to tease one nipple between his teeth. It pebbled against his tongue, and he blew hot air on her soft skin through the black bra.

She squirmed, deliciously rubbing his already hard cock. "Someone is sure about what he wants."

Passion flared deep within his soul, and his inner wolf howled. Could he have her without taking her? She'd given herself freely. He wanted to stay in the moment and not war with his demons. His skin rippled, and he fought the power of the other side.

With a frustrated grunt, he pushed off, tumbling until he rested on all fours. He remained in his human form but was quickly losing the battle. He hung his head over, panting. He couldn't risk it.

What the fuck? One moment, they were kissing hot and heavy and she thought she'd finally broken through whatever wall was imprisoning him. Mouth on her breast, cock pressed against her hip, the next step would be to get naked and take it to the next level, and then he reacted like all hell broke loose.

She watched him, heaving on the grass. Could he be sick? Shifting was different for each male. Maybe his was extremely bad. She moved toward him, placing her hand on his shoulder.

"Don't touch me," he snapped. "I'm a monster."

Instead of removing her hand, she smoothed, caressing his shoulder, offering soothing words of comfort. "It's all right. You won't hurt me."

"You don't understand." He lifted his head, his eyes glowing red—the color an even starker contrast against his pale skin. "I can't control it. My wolf controls me. And he wants you."

She shivered. From her feet on up, he sucked in her image. The sheer lust behind the look struck her to the core.

"He wants you with every DNA cell in my body. He wants to possess you."

"That doesn't scare me." Emboldened by her own wolf, she moved to stand in front of him. She hooked her thumbs in the front of her waistband and unbuttoned her jeans. The sound of the zipper lowering garnered his attention.

"You tell me what he wants. What do you want?"

She pushed her jeans down over her ass, bending slightly to accent her bottom, and stepped out of them, leaving her in a black thong. She ran her palms up and over her breasts, squeezing and lifting them.

His tracked her movements with his eyes. "You don't want to do that."

"Why? Because I might make you go over the edge? You might lose control? Maybe if you let your wolf have a little bit of what he wants, he'll surprise you, and you'll both feel better."

Taking two steps closer to him, her crotch was eye level for him. It was now or never.

"I can smell you, your desire. Fuck me." He

inhaled.

"I sure hope so."

Before she could react, he pounced, one hand snaking behind her to soften her fall, and his mouth delving into her pussy. He ripped her underwear full off and slid his tongue between her cleft. She arched up.

"Mmmm, nice. That feels good."

He reached up, bringing his fingers into her mouth. "Get them wet for me." His order came out a growl rather than a polite request.

In her mouth, she twirled her tongue over his fingers, sucking on them like she would suck on his cock. She put everything into it, so he'd get the overt hint. He brought his face close to hers, and his eyes smoldered.

"Naughty little she-wolf, aren't you? Do you know what I'm going to do with them now?"

He brought his hand between her legs, sliding his slick digits into her before returning his mouth to her clit. She squirmed against him, digging her fingers into his hair.

81

"Oh, Yas. That feels so good."

The pressure from pleasure built low in her belly, winding tighter and tighter. He licked and pumped his fingers, using the tip of his tongue to flick her clit, then folded it and thrust inside her pussy.

A low purring growl rumbled against her inner folds, and that added sensitivity pushed her over into climax. Her internal muscles contracted on his fingers, and he rubbed her, drawing out every last shiver.

She opened her eyes to the clear sky and stars. The moon glowed bright in the night.

He crawled next to her, sliding his hand over her outer thigh and closing her legs. Lying beside her, he brought her closer to his body, molding to her. His cock nudged her ass. Even through his jeans, his arousal was obvious. Smiling, she wiggled her bottom, rubbing her ass over his crotch.

"You best watch that. I'm barely controlling myself here."

"Who said you needed to stay in control?"

Experience with Yas so far said she needed to

push his limits to truly get a rise—well, of a different sort. Every time she brought him to the edge, he flipped the tables to retake the reins. She didn't exactly know what in his past made him so fearful, but he'd have to overcome it in order to truly be with her.

The moment he loosened his grip, she slipped from under his arm and sprinted just far enough away.

"If you want me, you'll have to catch me."

She closed her eyes, willing the power of the moon and the cycles of the earth into her body. Seamlessly as sliding on a change of clothes, her body morphed into wolf form. She shook, starting at her head and shimmying down to her tail. Her coarse black hair waved in the wind.

"Holy fuck! How'd you do that?" Yas stood, mouth ajar. "You turned, so easily. So fast."

She tilted her head. Not quite sure why it surprised him so. He needed to shift and follow her. A high-pitched howl erupted from low in her throat, and she lifted her head to free it into the night.

His eyes glowed as bright as the moon, and he

took a step toward her. She trotted a few feet, and then glanced back at him. Boyfriend was slow on the uptake.

Hands clutched at his shirt, he yanked off the material and discarded it. Next, he stripped off his jeans and boxers. Naked, standing before her, he looked more scared than she'd seen him before. She whined and nuzzled his leg.

"It's not as easy for me—the shifting. You make it look so easy."

Here's the thing. Either I tease the hell out of him and get him to shift and chase me, or I have to turn into my human side and talk him through it. After concentrating, she returned on her knees before him, his cock directly at face level.

Sliding her hand up his leg to cup his balls, she greeted him with a "Well hello, big boy."

The moment her palm touched him, he leaned forward, and the head of his cock brushed against her lips. "Mmmm," she said, licking the tip, and sliding her tongue into the slit. "I wonder what you want."

In one long swoop, she took him into her mouth

deep.

He groaned. "That might not help me at all, but it feels fabulous."

As she rose up, she stroked the silky skin, pumping her mouth on his sensitive erection. He'd been hard and awaiting some attention for a long time now. Before he stopped everything again, she wanted to work out some of the kinks.

With a light touch of her nails, she rubbed his perineum as she continued to suck his cock. He pumped his hips in rhythm to her movements and gripped the back of her head, holding her in place. She wasn't going anywhere. She was in it for the long haul.

"Oh, Tala."

His leg muscles flexed, contracting, and she knew he must be hovering on the precipice. With a firm grip, she increased the pressure until his body completely stiffened, and his cum flowed.

She slowed the stroke, coaxing him on, until his cock stopped pumping and she removed her mouth. "That's good, baby. Feel it," she said, with a last gentle caress.

The moment she let go, he collapsed on the ground, pulling her down with him.

"Wow, that was amazing." He leaned over, kissing her long and deep. "I didn't realize how much I needed that."

Elbows bent and hands tucked under his head, he reclined staring up into the galaxy. His entire body lost its tension.

"Are you ready to try to shift with me?" she asked. Making him shed his fear was the next step toward happiness.

He rolled over onto his side, studying her. "You're not going to let it go, are you?"

She shook her head. "Nope. You have to trust me. Merge the two beings of yourself, or else you'll never feel in control."

"Okay, let's do it." His voice took a resigned quality.

When he stood, he hung his head, and if he'd been in wolf form, she swore his tail would be tucked between his legs. She ignored the pouting.

"What happens when you shift? How do you control it?"

"I don't. Something either happens to me or in the environment. Usually I get mad and shift."

"You've never purposely thought about it and done it?"

"I've tried. I don't control it. It controls me."

How do I explain what it's like? I sure wish my brother were here to help me. "Listen, use visualization. Close your eyes and imagine taking your Wolf form—the feeling and the power. You're running across a meadow, paws pounding on the grass, and the wind ravaging your fur. Feel the energy."

With a sigh, he shut his eyes and concentrated. She watched him closely. His skin rippled, and, encouraged, she continued.

"See your body morphing from its human form into your Wolf. Your legs stretching out, your haunches curving, the shape of your face elongating, and the strength in your bones."

Each step, she walked through how it felt to

transform from her human shape into her wolf. The lucky males who had problems often had a father figure or male mentor to help guide them. If she had children, it was what she'd want to do. Teach them so they wouldn't be afraid. Not for the first time, she wondered about Yas's upbringing, and lack of training.

A single mom raising two shifters on her own in the big city? Maybe she didn't have the knowledge or resources to help him. Still, she should have tried something, reached out to the pack or another ex-patriot member.

"Arrrrgh." Yas threw his head back and roared. In one fluid movement, he went from human deep in concentration to his Wolf form. He stood before her, a magnificent creature with broad shoulders and thick, light-colored fur. He blinked his blue eyes at her, and bared his teeth in a grin.

He'd done it! Snout to the ground, he sniffed toward her, nosing her leg. She patted him away.

"Stop that, it tickles." She took a step backward.

With a nudge, he poked her thigh, and she

clamped her legs shut. Desire pooled in her belly, as she grew even wetter between her legs. He could smell her readiness. Higher still, he nuzzled right at her pussy, and she pushed him away.

Yas tilted his head to the side, elongated tongue hanging out as if he could taste her.

"Feeling frisky, are you now?" she teased, giving a few more moments to get a head start. Within a flash, she shifted and headed toward home. She wanted him all nice and proper, in bed.

Paws pounding the damp grass, she ran, taking in deep breaths, feeling at one with nature and the world. Nothing fueled her more. Her wolf connected with her psyche. One didn't exist without the other. She was lucky, being at peace with her dual natures.

A howl behind her drove her faster, and faster. The devil was on her tail, but this one she wanted to catch her. Would he ultimately be able to handle his bounty?

The porch light shimmered through the darkness, and Tala pushed, digging in. Her nails clattered against the wood steps, and she leaped over the last two. In two strides, she morphed into her human shape and entered the house. By the time Yas stepped onto the porch, she'd shut the door. In order to reach her, he'd have to shift again.

The next step in controlling his ability.

A loud thump hit the other side of the door, and the old wood vibrated. He scratched against the frame, and she heard a high-pitched whine.

"Fight it," she yelled, banging her fist on the door. "Don't let it win. If you want me, you have to be human again."

One more impact—she swore the old wood was about to give—and then silence. She held her breath, listening to nothing coming from the other side. Her heart rejoiced. Maybe, he'd won. Another bang resounded, and she jumped away from the door.

"Honey, Tala, open up. It's me," Yas called.

Nothing had ever sounded sweeter than his voice. Well, damn. He'd done it—with proper incentive.

Hesitation cast aside, she flung open the door. Chest heaving, he leaned against the wall, perspiration glittering on his skin. She drank in his sculpted chest all the way down to his yummy cock that looked oh so happy to see her.

"I thought you'd never get here," she said. "Are you ready to come inside and take me to bed?"

"Nothing I want more."

The moment he stepped over the threshold, his manner changed. The air charged with pheromones, and this time, Tala knew the race was really on.

Chapter Seven

With a burst of laughter that sounded more like a hooting owl, Tala dashed for the stairs. No way in hell, she'd let him win.

He bounded after her, and she retreated. Who was she kidding? She'd wanted him in her bed for too long already.

He grabbed her hand. "No more running, Tala. We're in this together, understand?"

The complete honesty in his eyes connected with her. With a gentle tug, he drew her against him, their bodies finding corresponding grooves, coming together inch by inch. He slid his hand under her hair, fingertips caressing her skin along the way.

Closer. And closer, until their lips were a mere breath apart.

"I want you," he said. "More than anyone ever before. More than that, I need you."

Needed. She didn't need to be taken care of, but someone actually needed her. It was a different feeling, but before she could say anything else, he stole the opportunity with a kiss.

Loving. As if all his emotions were behind that kiss. Sensation traveled through her body, starting in the pit of her stomach and branching out. Warmth infused every inch of her skin. Exhilaration. Here was the prize at the end of the race. Her heart pounded, and desire flared between her legs. He broke away from her, breathing heavy.

"Come on, upstairs," he said. "Let me make love to you, good and proper, in a real bed."

Something so simple, and yet his words stilled her heart. In all her meetings with men, she hadn't taken one to her bedroom. Part of it had been realistic. With her brother in the house, she didn't feel comfortable having sleepover guests. More so, she liked the control of not having to wait for the other to leave.

She'd let Yas into her home, and further into her heart.

After the work he had been doing in the house, her room now looked legitimate, complete with shelves for her books and porcelain wolf figurines. To celebrate, she'd even ordered new sheets and a bedspread.

She sat on the edge of the bed, tentative. Being indoors made her feel even more naked and exposed. Ground-in dirt caked her bare feet. And why not? They'd been rolling in the grass for hours.

"You want to get cleaned before we mess up these sheets?" she asked.

"Nothing I'd rather do," he said.

In the bathroom, she turned on the hot water and stepped inside. The luxurious spray enveloped her body like an invisible hug. Yas moved toward the rear of the stall, avoiding blocking the main stream. *Such a considerate guy.*

For being in such an isolated place, the one fringe benefit Tala's parents had spent money on was a big shower. Overhead, a large rain head covered most of the stall while a more focused one on the side worked perfectly for rinsing hair. A built-in bench acted as a safe place for relaxation.

In Tala's peripheral vision, she caught Yas

lathering up with the soap. The scent of vanilla-lavender permeated the enclosure and invigorated her. It was one reason why she liked the combination so much.

Her Wolf lover moved toward her, palms extended. He pressed up behind her, his cock sliding into the furrow between her legs, and he cupped her breasts with his frothy hands.

"Someone looks a little dirty," he whispered into her ear, before biting the lobe.

She ground her ass against him. "Are you sure you want me to clean up?"

"Not too much. I kinda like you dirty." He stretched his arms around her body, gliding his hands over her stomach, and dipping below toward her pussy.

As he swirled his fingers over her clit, tension built from her core and pulsed through her body. Tala's breathing hitched, and she leaned her head on his chest and kissed him, drifting between the sensations of the warm water and his even hotter body.

The thick hardness of his cock probed, searching for its own entrance into her heat.

"Place your hands on the bench and brace yourself," he directed. "You're so fucking hot. I have to take you now."

Without question, she obeyed. From behind, he plunged his finger into her pussy, stretching her, then guided his cock home. Inch by inch, he edged his way in, one hand resting on the small of her back, until he sank to the base. She rocked into him, loving every moment.

"Harder. Faster. Yes, show me how much you want me." Her words came out in short bursts. As he pounded into her, his balls slapped her ass.

"So much." He maneuvered their bodies until the stream of the water beat upon her clit, adding direct stimulation. All the while, he continued to thrust into her.

Every bit of lingering hesitation flowed down the drain, and she gave her pleasure completely over to Yas. At the thought of loving him, the orgasm ripped through her body. Not a slow build, but a complete grand slam. Her pussy clamped down on his cock.

"That's it," he murmured, encouraging her. "So hot. That's it."

And then he was thrumming inside her. His cock pumping out its own pleasure.

As their tremors ceased, Yas pulled out, and she turned within his arms. He kissed her eyelids. She rubbed her pelvis on his groin, enjoying the small aftershocks.

"Haven't you had enough?" he whispered into her ear, sending shivers through her body.

"Never."

A shift in the water pressure indicated it was about to turn cold. If they kept up these antics, she might have to ask him to install a larger water heater. She turned off the shower, and stepped out, handing him a towel and taking one.

"I thought you said you were going to make love to me all proper in a bed?" she teased, drying off.

"You wanton she-wolf." He snapped the towel at her thigh, causing her to squeal and jump. "See what you do to me? I couldn't wait."

"That's all right," she said. "I think we'll have plenty of time for that later."

Much later. Exhaustion set in the moment she settled into bed. Nude, he snuggled with her, one arm lazily slung over her hip.

Content. She could get used to the feeling.

***

In the light of the new day, Yas considered what had been happening the past few weeks. Tala snuggled closer to him in her sleep, and he luxuriated in the warmth of her body. Her tight ass pressed up against his groin, and he enjoyed the sensation.

I could get used to this. Very fast.

Who was he fooling? He was already used to it. He didn't like the idea of her staying at the B&B alone, with the events taking place. Broken windows were one thing, but the danger might escalate.

With an exasperated sigh, he rolled over, pulling away from the lover within his arms. The moment the cool air between them separated their bodies, she grumbled and scooted closer to him.

"Where'd you go?" she asked.

He slipped an arm under her neck and kissed her forehead. "Nowhere. I'm here. Just thinking."

She yawned, halfway covering her mouth. "What about? What's so vital to wake us up after last night?"

"Your brother. After all that has been happening, maybe you should call and fill him in. He might be able to visit for a few days and dispel the situation. If people think he's going to be around, then maybe that would kill these stupid sabotages."

"What do you mean my brother?" She drew closer to him, her face turned up. All he wanted to do was kiss away her anger, but he knew it would only make her madder. "How do you know my brother?"

He swallowed the lump lodged in his throat. "I told you about that…about meeting him."

She tilted her head to the side, and he watched her lips first purse and then part. "You. Did. Not. I would definitely remember you saying something about meeting Shilah. Why don't you tell me this mesmerizing story? Now." Without waiting for him to reply, she got out of bed and yanked on some clothes. "Downstairs."

So secure he'd follow, she didn't even glance back. Oh, and he did, feeling like his tail was tucked between his legs. She sat on the couch, legs crossed, and arms folded over her chest. If he didn't realize what was happening, or the fury beneath her outward calm demeanor, he might have believed they were sitting down for a light chat or tea.

Yas went to sit next to her, but her glare scared him away. He took the uncomfortable, overstuffed chair and scooted it closer to her. He wouldn't let her push him away. "Listen, Tala." He took her hand, hoping the physical connection would help bridge the gap between them. She held her hand stiffly. "It's no big deal. On my hike in, I ran into your brother."

She crooked an eyebrow and remained quiet. The silence lengthened, and he had to fill it. "I was looking for a place to stay, and he suggested I check out your bed-and-breakfast. He failed to mention quite how much upkeep it needed. That's it."

"Really? I have a hard time believing that. No, 'take care of my little sister, please'?" She pulled her hand away from him.

The tone of her voice cut through him. *Why the animosity?*

"Oh, sure. Do you think he'd send me up here to watch over you, maybe even sleep with you? Hell, maybe he thought we'd fall in love and get hitched. Then he really wouldn't have to worry about what happened to you. Right?"

"I wouldn't put it past him. You don't understand Shilah. He was used to constantly watching over me. Since he couldn't stand the thought of leaving Los Lobos and me behind, he did everything possible to make me go with him. But this one time, I refused. He couldn't persuade me. Very convenient for him to accidentally run into you and find a protector."

Yas barked out a laugh. "Protector. Do you think he expected me to jump into bed with you, too?"

"If that's what it took. Shilah's a pretty good judge of character. He might have taken you for a good guy." She stood up, brushing some nonexistent dust off her pants. No amount of smoothing it down would get rid of them. "Well, it's been fun. I appreciate all the work you've done here, but I'm not sure I'll need your services anymore."

"What are you saying to me?" He gritted his teeth. "We passed the employer-employee relationship a while ago." Physically, he moved closer. If she was trying to deny what they shared, he wouldn't let her.

"You made it very clear you were only here for a short time. Well, that deadline has passed. Have you found what you were looking for?"

He ran his fingers through his hair. "Argh. You're infuriating. Do you know that?"

Why the hell did I come here? I wanted information about my mother. But it wasn't like they were going to have her private journals, or suddenly, he'd get insight into what she was thinking when she left. Hell no. Instead, he got to see the beauty of the city, feel what it was like to live within a pack with others who understood what he was experiencing, and fall in love with Tala. Wolf or human form, he loved both sides of her.

"I've learned more than I could ever have hoped

or imagined," he said. With his fingertips, he tilted her chin up. "You've taught me more than anyone."

Chapter Eight

Damn, Yas wasn't making it easy for her. She insisted on standing on her own two feet, and even absent, her brother had to go and fuck this up for her. Yas was perfect. She never thought she'd meet someone like him in Los Lobos, and it had to take a stranger showing up out of nowhere to help her. Now, she'd learned it wasn't fate that brought him to her, but her brother. If only she could go back an hour in time and not find out. How could she look at Yas and not see her meddling sibling?

She'd about given up hope bonding with a mate, and when she'd least expected it, and least wanted it, it happened. Too bad the timing wasn't right.

He didn't understand. She saw the hurt in his eyes and had to close hers in order to shut it out. "I think you should find someplace else to stay."

She opened her eyes, taking in the firm set of his jaw. He looked away from her, and her heart panged at what she was throwing away. He was her one chance at happiness. How could her ideals make her turn away the man she'd fallen in love with? It made no sense. While her emotions screamed, her will turned to steel. She was determined to be independent, and she meant it.

No matter what the cost.

"Hmm, if that's what you want," Yas said. "That's one thing I don't do, stay past my welcome."

She watched his tight ass as he stormed upstairs, and listened to him stomp while packing his things. Tala sank into the couch. If she followed him, she'd end up saying she was sorry and asking him to stay. Pushing him into bed….

No way. Instead, she resigned to staying put. All too soon, he'd returned with his beat-up backpack slung over one shoulder. He hesitated at the door.

"If you need me, I'll be at Gee's for a few days until I figure out what I want to do." He swept his eyes across her body, and his hunger and pain cried out. When she didn't reply, he nodded and walked out of her life.

For no good reason, she'd chased him out.

Leaving Tala's place was one of the hardest things he'd ever done. As Yas walked off her property and down the road, he kept waiting to hear her chasing after him. Not only had he grown quite fond of their time together—living with her the past couple of weeks felt right, so easily they'd fallen into a routine—but he also worried about her safety in that big ol' house all alone. No wonder her brother didn't want her staying behind.

It was more than bad luck. Someone had purposely been sabotaging the construction. Thinking about her, an attractive woman—*his* woman— without protection, got his hackles all raised up.

Before he headed to Gee's, there was one stop Yas had to make first. He'd been avoiding it the entire time he'd been in Los Lobos. Now, when he was more down than ever before, why did he choose to go? Hell, he didn't get it. But if his time was about up in this small town, then he wanted to see the home he'd grown up in and his family had fled.

The house was located on the other side of town.

The farther he got away from the core of revitalization, the more rundown the remaining buildings became. Finally, he reached the end of the drive.

Wilderness encroached on the property. The main structure of the house remained, but it was missing the front door, and the windows had been broken out. Typical.

Could his family have moved out, and no one ever inhabited since? The gate hung on one rusted bracket. And he'd thought Tala's house had been unkempt.

A huge tree hung over the side of the house, and as he passed, Yas caught sight of chains and rubber submerged in the greenery.

His heart stilled. It couldn't be.

Memories of a tire swing or pushing his toddler sister while she giggled crowded his mind. How was it possible he'd forgotten? Until now.

Foliage crunched beneath his boots as he pounded a path to the front. He rubbed his palm against the trunk and gazed upward. It made a mighty fine swinging tree.

The sound of a bird hawking drew his attention to the house followed by a staccato of memories of his mom throwing plates at a man, screams, and fire. He tested the wood of the stairs and made his way up, blinded by the past and hopeful for the future.

Running his fingers over the bannister's peeling paint, he factored how much it would take to make the home hospitable again. After more than twenty years abandoned. He imagined his mom tending to the flowers. If left unattended, would they grow? The answer was yes, unbounded. And grow, and grow.

Inside, a damp muskiness filled his nostrils. So much of this wood would have to be knocked down and replaced. If he were staying in town, he'd probably start working on the house in his spare time.

In fact, who said he had to leave? Just because Tala didn't want him in her life didn't mean he had to run out of town with his tail between his legs. She might change her mind eventually, when she figured out that he wasn't the threat.

Seeing their old home threw him into even more

of a funk, and he had to get out of there quickly. Sure as shit he'd be doing some late-night visits to Tala's place to ensure everything was fine. Too soon, Yas arrived at Gee's Bar. One look at his face, no one asked many questions. After picking up a room key, he settled in upstairs. The joyful chaos of the bar was in stark contrast to the quiet solitude of where he'd been staying. He kept waiting to hear Tala's sweet voice as she called him to dinner. Instead, the rumbling of his stomach made him stop pouting long enough to go downstairs for a meal.

Gee acknowledged him with a nod, and the server slipped a plate of food in front of him. Paul raised his eyebrows and looked at the empty chair. Paul didn't utter a word, but Yas knew what the guy was asking. *Where's Tala?*

"Just me. She tossed me out. Damn that woman. She wants to be so independent, even when no one's trying to take her freedom away."

With a shake of his head, Paul commiserated with Yas. He lifted his palms upward and shrugged his shoulders.

"What am I going to do? Not hightail it out of this town and forget about her. She dug her nails into my soul, and now she won't be able to get rid of me so easily. I'll give her a little bit of breathing space, but I'm hoping she comes to her senses sooner rather than later."

After nodding in agreement, Paul pointed toward Yas's food. While the meals at Gee's were good, he figured he'd get mighty tired of them day in and day out if that was all he got. He should be eating beef potpie at Tala's about now and gazing into her sparkling eyes.

Damn it all. She had to hook him and then toss him like he was an underweight catch. As he ate, he eavesdropped on the various conversations happening. Most of the customers appeared to be pretty relaxed, but a group of three guys at the bar pounded the shots too quickly for his taste. In the space of half an hour, they'd ordered three rounds, and that was only what he'd seen. The tall, dark-haired guy on the end raised his hand at Gee, who shook his head and did a slash through the air with his palm. Yas recognized the universal signal for "done." They'd been cut off.

"Fuck that," the speaker for the group said with a snarl. He tossed some bills down and swept his hand across the bar, punctuating his words by knocking off the empties. The glasses crashed onto the floor. "We're outta here."

The jerk turned to survey the bar, probably checking out who was paying attention to the scene he'd created. The guy's nose and face looked flat, pushed in, as if he'd broken it too many times and hadn't bothered to get it reset. With such an attitude, it wouldn't surprise him if he'd been in a few altercations.

As Mr. Flat Face made eye contact with Yas, his eyes widened as if he recognized him. He elbowed the shorter dude next to him, and all three turned to check him out. A sense of unease soured Yas's gut. How could they recognize him? The only way would be to see him in town, and without Tala by his side, they probably figured out she was alone.

Gee came round the bar, arms crossed, and stared

down the threesome. Laughing, they headed out. He was reading too much into the situation. Just because he'd had the fight with Tala, now he saw potential danger everywhere. She'd lived in this town her entire life. Because he wouldn't be out there tonight didn't mean anything was going to happen to her, right?

No matter how he tried to convince himself otherwise, his gut clenched with determination. He pushed his plate aside and left some money to cover the bill on the table. By the time he reached the door, he was trotting. Paul swept up the broken glass, and Yas stopped for a moment.

"I'm heading out there to make sure she's all right," he said. "Didn't like something about those guys."

"There's a lot not to like about them," Gee agreed. He turned to wipe down the bar top.

Did that mean he was doing the right thing by following them? He could interpret the cryptic words a few different ways. No time to decipher the meaning, he stepped out.

The moon hung low over the rooftops, brightening the night's sky. The glow reached its lighted tendrils out, bathing him in its magical qualities.

For being so loud and obnoxious, the three guys were not to be found or heard. They reminded him of the frat boys he'd seen on campus. But, if they were as drunk as they'd seemed in the bar, they should still be fumbling somewhere close. Unless, they'd set off on a purpose.

His inner wolf growled and wanted to come out. He weighed the odds of shifting and unleashing his uncontrollable side. In wolf form, he'd move faster. Reflecting upon the calm lessons of Tala, he shut his eyes and willed his body to shift.

Nothing. He needed to do this now. A shiver crawled up his spine, and he shuddered in the cold night. He should be covered in fur about now, not freezing his white ass off in the middle of town.

He pictured flat-face guy, his head thrown back, laughing as he knocked the shot glasses off the bar, and the knowledge that passed between them when they made eye contact. Despite common sense telling Yas not to overreact, as sure as he could read the dude's mind, he knew he was out there and he planned to cause some sort of harm to Tala. Fury rocked through his veins. His she-wolf, and damn if he would let anything happen to her.

With a howl, pain ripped through his body and he bent over, panting. His shoulders stretched out, broadening, and his claws dug into the hard-packed earth. Within minutes, he stood in wolf form. Someone whistled from the direction of the bar, and he turned and caught Gee watching him. The guy gave a little salute before turning and sauntering inside. Whatever the fuck that was supposed to mean, he was done wasting time.

Chapter Nine

The old house settled, creaking and groaning. Tala lay in bed, listening to the sounds and doing a bad job of convincing herself it was all normal. She should be tired. She'd worked hard physically, and emotionally she was spent after Yas left. Pride kept her from chasing after him. But if he returned, she'd welcome him with open arms.

Hell, she was the one who'd run him off. She shouldn't be lamenting his absence.

She hated admitting that having him in the house had been nice. And it had helped. She wouldn't be lying there worried about every creak if he was in bed next to her. No, she'd be exhausted from some good loving.

Eyes shut, she drifted off into a semiconscious state, thinking about his wicked lips and even more talented fingers. A crash downstairs startled her awake. *What the hell was that?*

Panic rising, she waited for another sound.

115

Adrenaline pumped through her body. Something had woken her up, but she wasn't quite sure what it was.

I should go down and investigate. What if someone had broken in? It was stupid to chase Yas away. It would be one thing to have a home full of guests. It was quite another to be here alone.

Right when she pulled on her robe and slippers, the smell of smoke reached her. Fire? Yas had insisted she stock a fire extinguisher in her room. She'd thought it a waste of space. Now, as she grabbed it, she thanked him and his overzealous safety. She slid a flashlight into her pocket and headed downstairs.

A glow of red illuminated from the breakfast nook. One of the windows was smashed in *again*, and fire licked up the wood table and spread across the floor. Smoke billowed toward the ceiling and clung to her skin. She coughed, covering her mouth, and turned on the extinguisher. White foam burst forth, and she skidded in reverse before repositioning and bracing for the force. She aimed at the floor and swept the spray. The small patch in the kitchen went out fast, but more flames crawled in from outside. A broken bottle lay on the floor. Had someone thrown it through the window? *A Molotov cocktail? In Los Lobos?*

She'd have to go outside in order to attack the fire from there. Again, she wished Yas were there to help. She was an idiot. Sure, she could do all this solo. But if she didn't have to, why should she?

A rustling sound came from outside the window. She should have thought to bring a weapon for protection. Did she have something she could throw? She could always hit the guy over the head with the heavy metal extinguisher.

"Are you all right in there?"

Was that Yas's voice?

She caught a glimpse of blond hair and ran to the rear door. She threw the dead bolt and locks. He stood on the porch—soot marred his gorgeous face, and a streak of blood smeared across his fat bottom lip.

"What happened to you?" she asked, hugging him tight.

"Easy," he said, holding up his arms and

wincing. "You should see the other guys."

Other guys?

"Love to chat and make up, but can I have that?" He grabbed at the extinguisher and then went outside. She followed him, watching him stomp out a few last embers. "Good thing they were more drunk than determined."

"I can't believe someone would do this." With the back of her hand, she wiped the annoying wetness from her face, streaking grit over her cheek. *Great. Now imagine what I must look like, and what a superficial thought at a time like this.*

The smell of smoke stung her nose. Her knees caved, her vision blurred, and she collapsed. Strong arms gripped her waist as Yas steadied her against his sturdy body.

"Easy there," he soothed. "I've got you."

She twisted to face him, and he brushed smear marks off her face with his thumb.

"I don't understand what they could possibly want," she said. "What have I done to them? I don't hurt anyone."

"Sometimes it's not about you. It's about them. You're opening a bed-and-breakfast. Maybe people don't want a spot for outsiders to stay. Have you thought about that possibility?"

Could someone be sabotaging to keep me from opening?

"I'm not trying to bring in 'outsiders.' As we rebuild, those who fled or were forced to leave may return. I'm providing a place to stay. Look at you."

He raised an eyebrow. "What about me? Hopefully, you won't treat all guests the way you treated me."

"No, that's not what I mean. But I am worried about what happens when there's no one left to rent to."

"We make a pretty good team," Yas said. "When we're done here, I want to tackle my family's home, and maybe entice my sister to come for a visit. You could always be my handywoman."

She groaned in response, but he might be onto something. "As long as I don't have to use a hammer."

The heat of his body seeped through his clothes and hers, making it feel like there was nothing between them. The outline of his cock curved and thickened, pressing into her pelvis.

He separated from her, putting a minimal amount of space between their bodies, and tilted her chin up. "Look at me."

When her gaze connected with his, the tremors subsided. There were two options—she either had to keep fighting double and triple hard to prove she could do everything, or she could let this man enter her life, fully.

"I'm listening," she said.

"I have a feeling this streak of vandalism is over. After our physical discussion, they'll think twice about coming returning. And while I hadn't seen those guys before, they'd been at the bar. Gee would recognize them, and I'm sure that guy who dropped by to check me out would be interested in them, too."

Everything he said rang true. Although they'd tried, they hadn't stopped her.

Overhead, the clouds shifted and the moon broke

through. She glanced up, bathing in the beauty of la Luna.

"Come on, let's go inside," she said. "I'm going to need some help cleaning this place up. You think I might be able to convince you to stay a bit longer?"

With a whoop, Yas swept Tala off her feet and twirled.

"I knew it! You were only keeping me here for my handyman skills," he teased.

Once over the threshold of the house, he set her down. "I love you, Tala, and if I stay, I'd like it to be more official. If you'll have me."

"I love you," she said, sealing the declaration with a kiss. The thunder of her racing heart settled into a steadiness that felt right. "Plus, if you move into the master, we'll have one more room to rent!"

Epilogue

"I've got two gifts for you," Yas said, holding a wrapped package behind him.

Tala did her best to peek around his body. "What do you have?"

"Tsk-tsk. No cheating." He turned to the side, blocking her view. "One's something you can open, and the other is a little more fun, but not here. Which do you want first?"

"Humpf." Fake pouting, Tala crossed her arms. "I'll be patient. The one that's not here."

He lifted the box above his head. Gold paper glimmered and ribbons dangled, teasing. "You sure?" The laugh brought out a sparkle in his eyes that she'd come to love. "All right. I talked with Ryker, and he knew who the troublemakers hassling you were. The kid Clemet who hassled you out near the lumberyard. I guess he has an older brother. One you turned down in the past."

For the most part, Tala and her brother tended to

keep to themselves. She'd been tempted out to the swimming hole—a local hangout for teens—a few times. She didn't remember anything earth-shattering, but she recalled one guy getting a bit too touchy-feely under the water. She'd forgotten about it. Dumb teens. Obviously, he hadn't. *What a jerk.*

"Go on."

"Well, as punishment, he and his buddies will help clean up the mess they made." He grinned, showing off his teeth. "With supervision, of course."

"Good to hear. Don't expect me to make them sandwiches and lemonade." The business settled, her attention shifted back to the gift. "Now, how about the goodies?"

"My sister sent this for you," he said.

"It's so light." She didn't often receive presents with such pretty paper. She curled the ribbon around her index finger and pulled, watching it stretch taut and spring into shape. "It feels weird getting a gift from her. We haven't even met yet."

"You will soon enough. Sugar does things her way. Right now, she has no interest in visiting this 'backwoods town.' Her words. But she knows what you mean to me."

"Here I go." She flipped over the package and ripped the paper from the bottom, keeping all the top bows intact. With shaky fingers, Tala removed the lid of the white box. Beneath it laid folded purple tissue paper, held closed with a silver-embossed Congratulations sticker. One more layer.

She peeled back the closure, and a waft of lavender drifted toward her. She inhaled the scent, thinking about running through the wildflowers in the springtime. Beneath paper lay a gorgeous headband made from woven purple-and-white flowers.

"Oh, it's beautiful," she said, lifting it oh so carefully. Tears welled in her eyes.

"Put it on," he said.

"Are you sure? I don't want to hurt it."

He scoffed at her. "Sugar makes tons of these and sells them online. They're sturdy enough to ship, they're strong enough for you to wear."

Tala slipped the headpiece over her forehead, feeling almost like a princess. "How do I look?"

"Like a Wolf Goddess," he said. "And you better watch out, or else I'm going to claim you."

"It's about time," she said. "I thought you'd never get around to it."

"Seriously? I've waited, not wanting to push too much, too fast," he said, "and there was no need?"

Not waiting for her to respond, Yas pounced. The action so surprised her, Tala squealed. She never squealed.

Reverently, he caressed the sides of her face with his fingertips. "What do you say, my she-wolf. Will you finally let me claim you as my mate?"

"Yes."

His lips followed his hands. He kissed her cheek, jawline, side of her neck. Each seductive touch ratcheted her desire. Tala molded her body against his, hooking her heel over his calf so his cock pressed into the juncture between her legs. He ground against her, hips shifting beneath her hands.

"I need to taste you," he said. "Feel you."

She worked at the button and zipper of his pants, pushing the garment over his ass and freeing his cock.

He lifted the front of her dress, walking her in reverse against the wall. With one hand, he slipped her panties down, and she stepped out.

"So wet for me," he growled. "I can't wait to be inside you."

"Don't." She grabbed him and rubbed the hardness against her outer lips. He gripped her ass.

"Wrap your legs around me," he ordered.

Thrusting, he pushed into her, and she sank onto his cock in a fluid movement.

"Mine," he said.

A flash of pain at her neck as his teeth broke skin, and he sucked. They rocked against the wall, each delicious grind bringing her higher and higher.

"How I love you, Tala," he said, "Will you be mine?"

"Oh, yes."

The rhythm picked up, and her thigh muscles burned but not as much as the heat building within as her clit rubbed against the base of his cock, adding more friction. She'd never taken the blood of another during sex. Now, to complete their bond, she clamped onto his shoulder, right at the base of his neck. As her teeth punctured his skin, warmth and vitality filled her mouth and being.

Pleasure crashed through her, and her internal muscles spasmed as her climax hit. Yas's cock throbbed inside her, and Tala rode out the waves, being pushed farther into the wake.

As the adrenaline slowed, her lover—her mate—lowered Tala and smoothed out her skirt. She righted the wreath still on her head and reached to pick up her underwear. Yas grabbed them before her and gave her a playful smack on the ass.

"Maybe you should go without them today," he said, rubbing the spot. "And we can hope no new boarders show up."